Faeriely Tart

Beyond the Faerie Wall

Michelle Helen Fritz, E.A. Shanniak

CLEAR SPRING BOOKS LLC

Faeriely Tart: Beyond the Faerie Wall by Michelle Helen Fritz

featuring: E.A. Shanniak

Arabella Character Art: Liese's Art

Chapter Heading Art: Michelle Helen Fritz

Cover Design: Wanderlust Ink & Tome LLC

Crevan Character Art: Samaiya Art

Formatting: E.A. Shanniak

Proofreading: Cathey N.

Published by Clear Spring Books LLC of Clear Spring, MD

Dedication

from Michelle Helen Fritz

To Catherine Mary Ramble who was a storekeeper in a candy shoppe in Baltimore, Maryland during the early nineteen hundreds. My many greats grandmother, this tale is for you.

Author's Note

from Michelle Helen Fritz

Crevan has brought it to our attention that you may better enjoy his tale, if you knew how to properly pronounce his esteemed name and the meaning behind it. So...you're most welcome.

Crevan
Origin: Irish
Meaning: Fox
Sound: Crev-an

Contents

Chapter One

Faerie Tarts

No creature in all of Faerie ever baked quite like Mister Crevan Sunbriar, whose confections were highly praised and priced at exorbitant rates. His flour was spelled to rise with perfection, and the magnificent scents that wafted along the air of his shoppe, *Faeriely Tart*, enticed his patrons to linger. They relaxed into the lattice-backed chairs that were settled under the polished wooden tables, and filled their bellies. His faerie fare was sumptuous, and yet, no matter how much one consumed, they never gained weight; this was a good thing as the patrons entered and exited through a small quaint door. The shoppe was a simple but charming cream and periwinkle cottage with a stepping stone walkway. To the ignorant eye, the cottage was nothing extraordinary, not when Faerie boasted castles, haunted dwellings, and ravishing waterfalls; the real splendor of the confectionery revealed itself to guests only once they stepped through the entrance.

The focal point of the entire establishment was the flowing waterfall of chocolate that rained down from the roof's beams to flow like a river, leaving splatters of cocoa droplets along the rocky edge of the attraction. The pool of enticing liquid pleasure swirled in circles as delightful aquatic creatures fashioned from the richest of cocoa beans swam under its dark surface. If one watched the chocolate pool long enough, they would spy the creatures leaping from its depths and arcing in graceful lines to splash back into their chocolatey home.

Mammoth statues of marzipan sculpted to resemble frolicking faeries with fluttering butterfly wings, tails that ended with tufts of hair, sharp toothed-smiles and sometimes bore elaborate curved horns or antlers danced among enchanted castles. Cornucopias of fruit stood sentry along the side walls. A faerie could hide among the figures, tricking their friends when playing a game of hide-and-seek, which only the most enchanted customers longed to do after consuming the charmed fruit-filled pies.

With upraised dark brows, the proprietor, Crevan, stood amid his gingerbread-colored walls and surveyed his patrons. A trio of faeries with pearl-white feathered wings sipped their hot chocolate with relish. The wisps of steam from their treats drifted into the air to coil above their golden curls, creating phantom horns, which was just one of the many perks clientele would receive from devouring his edible treats.

Faeriely Tart's offerings each possessed their own magical effect. After consuming certain treats, patrons delighted in changing forms from faerie to monster, lion, goat, or tiny firefly. Or, if they were feeling insignificant, eating toffee ensured they gained weight, only to rapidly shed it again upon tottering around for a bit. Chewing the nonpareils could instantly change a patron's hair, eye, or skin color. If one wanted to feel the bewitchment of adoration, they could nosh on the peppermint sticks. If one were ill, the chocolate cake was a tried and true cure-all.

Onto the dark floor, tendrils of amber light fell from the marzipan window panes where colorful scenes of confectionery sweets had been decorated with swirls of decadent icing. Along the shelves of the walnut-colored walls were various glass containers in shades of burgundy, navy, and emerald, each filled to its brim with baked treats. Every craving of sugary goodness could easily be satiated by the plethora of licorice, gummy shifters, chewy caramel, taffy, and even butterscotch.

Walnut counters gleamed under the teal faerie lights that floated in the air, highlighting the wonders of each corner and crevice of the shoppe. Under a dome of oblong glass that spanned the entirety of the main counter were silver trays bearing baked goodies in a mix of fudge, scones, tarts, chocolate cakes, red velvet cupcakes, tea cakes, and any tasty morsel one could possibly dream of.

Crevan smugly beamed at his baked goods. It had taken him years to perfect baking, longer still to perfect baking with magic, but now his skills were unparalleled. He reached into the toffee container and popped one of the delicacies into his mouth. Crevan closed his eyes as the sweet, nutty taste burst with flavor over his tongue.

Exquisite!

But wasn't *everything* he did these days exquisite?

The gold bell hanging over the door to his shoppe jingled. Crevan's auburn-haired head snapped in the direction of the sound as he watched a gaggle of faeries enter. They gathered around the large table at the northern end of the shoppe at the furthest table from the waterfall, and each took a seat. Edible potted sugar-coated flowers dotted the walls beside them. Crevan grabbed the handwritten cream-hued menus from their elaborate brass holder at the end of the walnut counter and took them over to the group.

"Sir, you must get rid of that blasted crow lingering outside your confectionery," an elderly female faerie snarled at him.

Crevan tilted his head to the side as he regarded the female. Her brown curls were piled high atop her head as if she hoped the added height would give her a semblance of importance. Her empire-waisted burgundy dress hugged her plump figure. Crevan took a quick glance at the table, noting that they *all* resembled this delightful fae with the same hairstyle, gown, and arrogance. He had never had the *pleasure* of these ladies in his establishment before.

Her haughty blue eyes narrowed on him. "Are you listening to me?" Before Crevan had the opportunity to answer, the female commented to her companions, "He must be deaf."

"Or daft," another lady chimed in, eyeing him with disgust.

Ten sets of eyes warily took him in. Every inch of Crevan was a testament to his elegance—his polished Hessian boots, pristine black trousers, emerald vest with pearl buttons, matching black tailcoat, and a white lace cravat tied to resemble an unfurling rose. It might have been true that in his soul resided a clash of whimsy and chaos, a deeply dark, creative heart. But wasn't that what made beings so captivating? The differences between outside appearance and what lingered within? And unless one took the time to really dig, no one would ever uncover what it was that made Crevan tick. He wasn't certain that even *he* knew the secrets that drove him.

"My sincerest *apologies*, dear patron," he replied with a grin, handing her the menu. Crevan's fox tail twitched merrily, rising behind him like a waving flag at having insulted her with a heedless apology, for faeries hated the human custom of 'thankfulness'. "Whatever creature resides outside shall remain so. Unless it comes inside, I've no need to quarrel with nature. You, however, are welcome to do as you see fit." Crevan bowed low at the waist as his arm swept into the air before him.

The female fae snorted. "I'll take a hot chocolate and a King's Apple Tart."

"Very good," he replied, turning his attention to the lady beside her.

Much to his surprise, all the ladies requested the same. Getting ten of the same treats made his task much easier, even if he found boredom in the simplicity of the chore. Crevan's real happiness was found in his kitchen, creating his sweets. Greeting his customers and retrieving their fare left him feeling indifferent, even if a part of him relished in their enjoyment of his creations. Gathering the menus from the table into his long-tapered fingers, Crevan turned on his heel.

Crevan retreated to his place behind the counter. He riffled through a cabinet and withdrew the green-apple-decorated plates. He then slid the glass door open, bringing the silver-trayed tarts to rest atop the counter, and he gingerly set each tart upon a plate and sprinkled his special crystalized sugar on each.

That shall fix their foul behavior. A shiver gleefully danced up Crevan's spine. His sugar was spelled to boost the mood, turning the sourest of fae into smiling simps. He stared for a moment at one of the tarts before adding just a sprinkle more of the spelled sugar. *A little dash more might do that one some good.* He grinned. *A little* positivity *and* kindness *will go a long way for her.*

Carrying the laden delicacies with expert ease, he disbursed a treat to each patron along with their requested beverage. Crevan stealthily waited off to the side and eagerly anticipated witnessing the elderly female take a bite of his treats. Watching her eyes light up upon tasting the tart made Crevan beam, and his lips twisted into a smile.

He swaggered his way back to his spot behind the counter, whistling a merry tune.

His fingers strummed on the countertop as he deliberated about making a new kind of tart. The project would take him a while to concoct, and he wouldn't be free until after the late afternoon rush, which wouldn't hit for another couple of hours.

Sour sand plum tart with a hint of mint, he thought, his tail twitching. *But what about the effect?*

A rapping upon one of the windows caused Crevan's head to jerk in the direction of the unwelcome interruption. From the tip of its beak, a silly little crow held an acorn, banging the nut against the window. The crow turned its keen golden eyes every which way, attempting to peer through the spelled marzipan-paned glass. Crevan was amused by the little bird's antics as it busily went about its day.

After a time, Crevan slunk back to where the condescending female fae was happily seated. When he reached the table, unnoticed, he gathered the soiled dishes with ease. The females all twitched giddily in their seats, leaning forward to hear the latest town gossip. Lately, humans had found their hidden forbidden-to-cross Wall and were practically leaping over in search of fortune and glory, only to find themselves stuck in a land unimaginable to their minds. While he was collecting bramble berries, Crevan had happened to come across a female mortal searching for her brother, but he seriously doubted *that* was the reason she was truly there.

"I'll take another tart," one of the younger and slimmer faeries to his left ordered.

Crevan nodded before replying, "As your waistline wishes."

The female giggled, batting her long chartreuse lashes at him. Crevan shuddered; *butterfly fae... ewwww.* He had respect for all of the creatures in Faerie, but some were more attractive to him than others, and it wasn't that he was prejudiced per se. It was more an acute aversion to wings that fluttered and flew at him. He could stand being in the presence of a being with wings as long as he wasn't their sole focus.

"Did you hear about the latest human?" chortled the outspoken elderly female from earlier. "She got turned into a bird for trying to steal the king's Wayfinder berry!"

Another faerie tittered into her napkin. "Serves the imp right! The Wayfinders are strictly for the king!"

"Poor dearie," the chartreuse-lashed fae said, clucking her tongue. "She must have been desperate to resort to stealing."

"No desperation should result in stealing," an owl-beaked fae snarled. The male had been sitting at a corner table all morning reading the *Faerie Times* and sipping from his cup of moonroot tea.

Crevan nodded his own agreement. Stealing was worse than the dreaded *politeness* the humans so *enthusiastically* displayed. If the mortal got turned into a bird for stealing, it served her right. In his mind, she should be on the other side of The Wall as a bird and not locked in their realm, free to thieve from unsuspecting fae. It was another of the disagreeable rulings of their esteemed monarch.

Making his way through the swinging door to the kitchen, Crevan unloaded the dishes from his arms into the copper sink. After washing his hands with foamy soap, he returned to the shoppe display counters and fetched a new dish. Crevan loaded another apple tart onto the plate, topping it with a light green confectionery powder bespelled to give that eyelash-batting butterfly a peppery edge. He never had a terrible encounter with butterfly fae; he just loathed how they were all so unbearably chipper...and, of course, there was the whole wing thing. Crevan's lips curled with distaste.

Chapter Two

Winter Wonderland

Why was it that one berry, the overwhelming desire to taste it, had landed Arabella in an impossible situation? What had driven her to steal that ripe, juicy fruit when everything within her had been screaming at her to run away and never think of it again? Why, oh why, couldn't she have listened to her conscience? In the midst of a winter wonderland with the snow softly falling, a vibrant green vine flourished. Attached to the greenery were the most delectable-looking raspberry-hued berries that had made her mouth instantly water. The fact that the vine grew clinging to a stone wall, despite the frigid landscape of the Faerie King's barren garden, should have filled her with terror. Even now, the phantom scent of the berries filled her nose, and her tongue longed for the burst of flavor to dance along with her taste buds. Hanging her head, Arabella let out a sigh that ended in a high-pitched caw.

Of all the vilest creatures to be turned into, why had the king chosen *a crow* to be her fate? The compulsion to capture and hoard shiny things was almost too much to bear now. If she had thought her desire for the bewitching berry was beyond reason, her newfound attraction to anything that sparkled was a living nightmare. Buttons, cufflinks, jewels, anything that glinted in the sunlight and that Arabella could easily fit into her beak became her obsession, even after she laid atop the treasure nest she had built in the cottage eaves, keeping her safe from the snowflakes that dotted the thatched roof.

When she could pry herself away from the over-laden nest, Arabella tried to solve the puzzle that plagued her. Actually, there were several at the moment, which one would expect for a mortal trapped in the land of faeries...but just now, her attention was on the cottage and its inhabitants. It was perplexing that guests came to stay for endless hours and left with happy smiles and high spirits. Just what occurred in the cottage? Was it some sort of business or lodging or, gasp...a house of ill repute? Was that where she had decided to make her new home? As an orphan, she had lived in many unsavory dwellings with sinister plans afoot. It was a miracle that she had never been tampered with.

There was an unreadable air surrounding the faerie that most often came and went through the cottage door. Arabella was good at reading people, a skill that had always served her well. But here in

Faerie, her skills were useless. To even attempt to get a real understanding of the realm or its residents was an impossible feat.

Arabella was accustomed to taking care of herself; she'd been doing so for as long as her memory stretched. She'd been wrong to trust the hooded figure who promised her dreams would come true if only she would follow him over The Wall. The forbidden, formerly hidden, Wall. Once she had truly seen it, she could never again unsee it.

Twilight was calling upon the realm as unbelievable petals of pink and purple blossomed across the horizon. Only here in Faerie were the colors, the smells, everything, just *more*. It was a paradise much as a spider's silken web was for the unsuspecting fly who flew too close and had been caught in a lingering death... Danger lurked in every direction.

The dazzling and hauntingly beautiful faerie exited the cottage as a blustery wind nearly ripped the top hat from his head. While one hand gripped the doorknob, the other secured his topper by latching onto the brim. When the ardent breeze died down, the fae gentlefaerie released a sigh and let his hand fall back to his side. Redirecting his attention back to his task, he inserted his brass key and twisted the tumblers in the lock. Dropping the key in the left pocket of his trousers, the dapper faerie reached a hand up to adjust his top hat once more. He swung his walking cane out in a circular loop as his boot steps hammered over the stepping stones. A thick copper tail rose from the seat of his trousers to swish back and forth behind him. This wasn't the first time Arabella had viewed the fae feature as she watched his comings and goings from the cottage. She had formed the conclusion that he was either a squirrel or a fox and wasn't quite certain which one his Unseelie form took.

So, where was he going now? Curiosity sunk its talons into her mind. Arabella stood from her nest, flapping her obsidian wings and craning her neck to keep watch on the faerie's progress. Rising into the air, she kept a safe distance from him as he walked deeper into the forest, doused in a white so pristine that it made her eyes narrow to slits. He was a faerie on a mission and so must she if she wanted to satiate her curiosity, despite the biting wind that slid through her feathers.

The faerie briskly trudged over the fallen snow, crunching ice under his boots. He occasionally ducked below low-hanging tree branches overbrimming with snow wary of the threat of snow dumping upon his head. When the trees began to thin, a clearing was revealed, and in that clearing sat a building constructed of clear glass. Through the walls, she spied potted greenery and towers of lattice fencing. Flora crept and twined along trellises.

Arabella knew next to nothing about growing things or what they were. She was at a loss when the faerie produced another key and unlocked a translucent door. He entered and crouched in front of one of the pots. He positioned his walking cane under his arm and removed small silver-plated shears attached to a chain that hung from his waistcoat pocket. Taking small clippings of the green plant, he delicately placed them into the folds of a silk handkerchief.

As her wings drew her through the entrance and nearer to him, she was surprised when he leaped to his feet and faced her. With a swat of his hand, his palm nearly made contact with her satiny wing.

"Be gone with you, foul fiend!" he cried out in alarm.

With an outraged caw, Arabella had to right herself mid-air. She was still getting used to her wings and the mechanics of how they functioned. Her heart seized in her chest, and her breaths came in soft pants.

Scoffing, she flew to a nearby tree branch with golden leaves. "You didn't need to swat at me," she cried, even though he couldn't understand her due to the hex she suffered. Since becoming cursed to forever take the form of a blasted bird, no one but another animal could speak with her. Not even fae in their Unseelie form could converse with her.

Arabella flapped her wings in vexation and settled onto the tree branch. Her attacker eyed her with annoyance, then moved to another plant, carefully cutting snippets off and putting them into the silken handkerchief. Arabella's tiny feet moved her down the tree branch to observe. She couldn't help letting out a long yawn; flying was simply too exhausting, especially when one was battling the wind currents.

"You really are quite the little nuisance that my patrons prattled on about!" the grumpy fae snarled. "Your presence is unwelcome. This is my private atrium."

She huffed, her feathers becoming puffed from irritation, but she didn't deign to give him any attention. Arabella hopped to the tip of the branch, keeping an alert eye on him. Since becoming a bird, her sense of direction was vastly improved; however, she still couldn't find her way to the human realm, which was challenging when she was mid-flight on a mission to swipe a particular treasure from an unsuspecting being.

The intrusive thought of home made her pause. Was the mortal world truly ever her home? Since going to the orphanage at the tender young age of six, Arabella was quickly glossed over for adoption, with the families always choosing the prettier girls, and more often the boys, over her. She had heard one lady remark that her hair was too dark and her eyes a bewitching emerald green, qualities that forever cast her as an *Unwanted.* The Unwanted were those poor creatures whose parentage was dubious and clearly came from another race, a not quite mortal being. As Arabella aged, she was then looked over for being too mature, too set in her ways, wild and unchristian. She did laundry for barely any wages and worked wherever she could at night for leftover bread crumbs. It wasn't until this past spring that she began carrying a knife on her person in case undesirable male attention struck. In abject desperation, she'd resorted to stealing food: an apple here, a small loaf of bread there, just something to satiate the sourness in her stomach and keep her from starving. So, was that abysmal place home?

Arabella shook her head. *If I must choose, this is more like home. At least as a blasted bird, I'm not starving anymore.*

The faerie took a wide berth around the tree while glaring up at her.

"What's your problem?" she squawked at him when she could take no more.

"Stay there, foul creature," the fae hissed. It struck her that since she didn't know his name, *Grumpy Trousers* seemed to be a perfect moniker.

Arabella flapped her wings at him, which seemed to unsettle him even more. Grumpy curled his lip and walked briskly away. *He loathes birds*, she mused. Arabella leaped off the branch and flew directly at him, coming close to nicking the hat that perched on his auburn head. The fae waggled his walking cane in the air at her, calling her all sorts of creatively vile names. She laughed as she taunted him, flying from the atrium to watch Grumpy complete his errand.

The grumbling faerie eventually strode through the door, locking it behind himself with an irritated harrumph. His steps soon carried him back through the forest and to the cottage door. Arabella tilted her head to the side, silently watching him as she trailed in his wake.

Grumpy's dark brows furrowed as he dug for the key in his pocket. His right hand gingerly held the handkerchief, which now boasted a pretty dark blue flower as well as the earlier clippings.

Just what or who is he keeping locked inside?

Arabella moved closer, hopping along the edge of the roof. A dragonfly burst from the gutter, disturbing the peaceful setting. Arabella clicked her beak, startled by the bright pink creature who seemed to be misplaced and unsuited to survive in wintertide. The bug's long, oval, translucent silver wings flapped thousands of times in a single second. The bug hissed, spouting fire from his bright pink dragon maw.

Arabella ducked to avoid the tiny but mighty blue flame and flitted around the creature. "My apologies. I didn't know you resided there."

"Don't apologize, you insolent bird!" the insect huffed, blowing more fire in her direction.

The dragonfly turned directly toward Grumpy Trousers. Arabella did the same. The faerie accidentally dropped his bronze key, muttering curses under his breath. The blue flower sparkled as it neared the ground, catching her eye. Arabella hopped to the very edge of the roof, her beak clicking with desire for the pretty flower that was now shining like a thousand tiny diamonds as snowflakes coated it.

"That's mine!" the dragonfly yelled.

The dragonfly zipped past her, dive-bombing toward the male fae and spouting fire. Grumpy yelped, swatting at the creature. Arabella launched herself into the air, going to Grumpy's aid. She swooped down, catching the bug with her claws.

The bug thrashed in her grasp. "Let me go, you villain!"

"Don't bother coming back here!" Arabella snapped, flicking the creature away from her.

"You can't tell me what to do!" it shouted, diving straight for her.

Arabella dodged out of the way of the blue fire. The dragonfly spun around, making another pass at her. Its flames singed the delicate skin of her left foot. Arabella gasped from the blinding flare of pain that zipped lightning along her nerve endings. Cawing in pain, she hurriedly flapped away from the danger.

"Oh, no, you don't!" The dragonfly snarled.

Arabella rolled in the air just in time, catching the dragonfly in her right claw. "Leave!"

"You leave!"

Arabella squeezed her claw tighter, and she clacked her sharp beak. "Leave here!" she demanded, feeling braver than she'd ever been before.

"As you *please*!"

Once again, Arabella flung the dragonfly out of her claw, and carefully tucked her injured foot below her, flying back toward her nest. Perching at the edge of the cottage, Arabella lifted her left foot to inspect it. The dragonfly's brutal flame ruined her beautiful feathers. She hissed, setting her foot down and wishing that she had the healing ability faeries possessed.

"Nasty, insufferable dragonfly," Grumpy sputtered, looking around for him, and then searched the ground for his fallen key.

Arabella tilted her head, looking down for it as well. Bronze wasn't as shiny as copper or brass, though his key appeared to be quite nice. Arabella took to the sky again to get a better look despite her pain. She flapped around to face the cottage when she spied the key in a dark potted plant.

"Here it is!" she exclaimed as happiness warmed her heart. "I found it."

"Oh, not you again!" Grumpy rolled his amber eyes. "You've caused enough trouble."

"I have not!" she protested as her enthusiasm deflated. Arabella hopped up on the edge of the pot. "I saved you!"

Grumpy turned around, spying the key in the pot. "Oh," he said, fetching the key. "Good on you."

"Yeah, good on me *now*. Too bad you can't understand me!"

The male fae tilted his head and narrowed his eyes on her. "I suppose for helping me, I should help you," he said, sighing irritably and rubbing at the skin on the back of his neck. When his gaze landed on the blue flower, he bent to retrieve it.

"I'll believe it when I see it," she taunted.

In all she had encountered thus far in Faerie, the fae were nothing like what they pretended to be. They were much, much crueler.

Chapter Three

Bath Bugs

Crevan hunched his shoulders forward as he bitterly eyed the injured bird. Was it really his fault that it had been hurt? Perchance minding its own business would've served it much better. But he was a gentle-faerie, and as it seemed, a good deed was always delivered hand-in-hand with a punishment; he might as well get this entire misery behind him. Unlocking the door, he allowed it to hang wide open and waved his hand in the air.

"Mind your manners and fly straight to the kitchen. Don't dawdle or gawk at the wonders within. You are sorely in need of a bath, and I do think a few nibbles of the chocolate cake and perhaps a lick of the macaroons will set you to rights. My customers won't relish feathers in their fare, so do use care." He stood rigidly in place and waited to see what the crow would do.

The frustrating bird spread her wings, tucked her legs beneath her, took to the ether, and flew in as instructed.

Crevan dusted the snowflakes from his shoulders, kicked the slush from the toes of his boots, and removed his greatcoat and his topper, giving them a vigorous shake to force the errant flakes to fall away. Then, he followed the bird through the door. He watched the crow soar through his shoppe with its mouth agape, and he even thought he heard the sounds of its gurgling stomach. He didn't fault the animal's reaction to what he had built. Crevan's creations were mesmerizing, and the bird's clear appreciation of his talent raised the creature in his esteem.

"I'm so very pleased that even a *creature* such as yourself can manage to follow even the simplest of instructions so well." Crevan icily voiced his thoughts.

Once his steps took him into his kitchen, he wasted no time in hanging his things upon a cloak stand and removing his kidskin gloves. Crossing to the cabinet above the sink, he opened it and retrieved a tiny vial of blue liquid. Collecting a daisy-patterned tea kettle, Crevan poured its contents of boiling water into the copper sink. When he added a drop of the blue liquid from the vial, wisps of periwinkle-blue steam rose into the air, warming his cold nose. He stepped away from the sink and met the bird's eyes.

"Into the makeshift tub, you go! I haven't all evening to accommodate you. So please be tidy as you speedily bathe."

The crow descended from the it's perch atop the cupboards and sank into the sink. It floated atop the water and stretched its wings as wide as the fowl could to let them soak. The bird's beady eyes squeezed shut in pleasure as it bobbed its head, cackling in pleasure. The drop of healing potion did its job, and her burns were soon forgotten.

Crevan eyed the strange animal, wondering how a bird was so observant and obedient. With great care, it ducked its head under the water and splashed itself. Dirt floated off its obsidian wings, giving it a new shine he hadn't even noticed. Granted, Crevan despised winged things, but this bird had a beauty to it which he hadn't cared to take notice of until now. The crow had a green glint to its wings that shimmered magnificently in the light.

Crevan snapped his fingers. "The shimmer of your wings has given me an idea," he told the bird. "My next creation shall have a likeness to your wings."

The crow squawked at him.

"I'm glad you agree," he said, holding out a dish towel. "Now, caw once if you're a male crow and twice if you're female. I would hate to upset you by calling you something you aren't."

The crow rose from the sink, shaking its body as the spray of water droplets landed on Crevan's hand, making him cringe and curl his lip. Hopping into the soft folds of the towel, it cawed twice.

"Ah," he said, awkwardly patting the animal dry. "Are you, by any chance, a human girl? Caw once for no, twice for yes."

She cawed twice as she rubbed her head against the towel.

Crevan nodded. He wasn't one to meddle in whatever punishments the king gave; however, he felt obligated to the piteous mortal to help. She saved his head from getting singed by a terrible dragonfly and found his key, never mind that she has proven herself a nuisance to his customers. Crevan took a step back, swiping a hand over his face.

"Stay here," he instructed, stepping away from the sink for a moment and then striding from the kitchen straight to his display counters.

He rummaged through his jars of bewitched confections, searching for his special 'Whisper Winds.' A long time ago, a mouse had wandered into his establishment. Crevan instantly despised the horrid little creature, but this one was different. Instead of it sporting the beady black eyes he had come to know of mice, this one had deep teal orbs. Intrigued, he decided to help the creature by concocting a spell to allow the mouse to communicate with him without Crevan having to shift into his fox form. It was such a bothersome thing to put forth the effort to shift forms. He rather enjoyed his life on two legs instead of four. His bushy tail twitched behind him, reminding Crevan that that was one thing he had never sought to mask away. His tail often told his mood, and when he was overheated while concocting his creations, it would fan cooler air his way. As far as he was concerned, his tail was marvelous.

Perhaps, Whisper Winds will allow me to communicate with the crow? Locating the spelled powder, Crevan dipped two fingers into the navy-colored jar, withdrawing a few pinches of the substance, then pushed the lid back on top. Turning, he hastened back to his kitchen and sailed through it to stand before the enchanted fowl.

"Hold still," Crevan instructed. He sprinkled the sugary magic over the beak of the crow and watched on as magenta sparks lit upon the ebony feathers. "Now, if you are enchanted, try speaking. This spell should allow you to talk."

"Thank you," the crow cried happily, working her beak around the vowels and consonants. "Thank you, thank you, thank you!"

"And you're definitely *that* human," Crevan said knowingly, rolling his eyes. He reached for a dish towel and wiped his fingers free of the magical sugary residue. "Don't you dare thank me again! *Ughhh*! Human politeness is abysmal."

"I could say the same for the fae arrogance."

Crevan barked a laugh, tossing the towel down onto the counter. "Now you're catching on. Shall we discuss your role as we break this enchantment?"

"What role is that to be?"

"Just wait there. I shall gather the proper treats to cure you," he said as he briskly walked from the kitchen, its swinging door swooshing behind him.

Crevan's boot steps sounded across the marbled tiles until he reached the glass counter and slid the door aside. Using tongs, he selected a mint macaroon and turned to collect a cloth napkin to deposit it on. Swiveling back to the glass dome, he retrieved the chocolate cake and set it down with a thump on the counter. Crevan reached into the drawer just under the counter and pulled out a server to remove the smallest slice of the gooey chocolate cake. That, too, he set upon the napkin. There was no use wasting a plate that would have to be washed. He placed the server into a small basket set under the counter, then straightened to set the stand with the remaining chocolate cake back into the cold storage.

Every evening, once the last patron exited the confectionery, the entire shoppe prepared itself for a rest. The glass dome counter became colder to preserve the fare, the chocolate waterfall heated to cook out any unsavory bits, and tiny dwarfs scurried from a hidden hatch between the kitchen and the serving area. He didn't usually see the dwarfs, and thankfully so, as they sang the most nonsensical melodies while they cleaned his establishment. The best part for him was that he paid them their wages in chocolate. The little creatures especially coveted the coconut bonbons.

Carefully, Crevan picked up the napkin and held it between his two hands, then made his way back to the kitchen. When he came through the swinging door, he nearly dropped the treats as his eyes widened in horror. The blasted crow was sprawled out atop his counter, perfectly still, while nasty little ants marched a path up its obsidian wings.

"Ants! In my kitchen! Oh no! This will never do. Out, out, *out!*" Crevan screeched as he rushed forward to drop the napkin and its contents down onto the counter. He whirled toward the crow and her army of insects as lava flared through his veins and his skin heated. His tail was waving furiously back and forth behind him.

"What is wrong with you?" The crow yelled up at him with indignation, puffing up her chest feathers.

"Me? *You*! You get them out right now! Once the beastly little menaces make themselves comfortable, my kitchen, my *life,* will be in shambles! I cannot abide messiness in my kitchen!" With a grimace, he lifted the crow and the infestation into his hands and shuddered so violently he almost dropped them; whether caused by the feel of the wings or the terror of the ants, he wasn't certain.

Crevan ran forward, out the swinging door, rounded the main counters, and kept going. A nasty stumble had him looking down to spot one of the dwarfs who was looking back up at him, his little magenta hat askew on his ebony-haired head.

"The door!" Crevan cried out, using his elbow to motion to the cottage door.

The dwarf blinked back at him with a frown.

Crevan rolled his eyes before saying, "Yes, *my apologies!*" Dwarfs were almost as notorious as mortals when it came to their feelings and inane politeness.

Hickleburt, or perhaps it was Henwick, righted his hat and then took off with a run, which instantly had the little thing huffing and puffing. Crevan's brows drew together as he wondered whether the dwarf would keel over or make it to the door. They didn't have much further to go.

"Murray? Murray!"

Murray reached the door, fumbled on his tiptoes to unlock it, and then flung it wide open. Crevan sprinted past him and through the door, over the pavers, and straight to the lane. Bending forward, he deposited the crow and the ants onto a vacant flower pot, ardently shook his hands, then stood straight. Backing away, he eyed the creatures with disdain.

"Was that absolutely necessary?" asked the crow as she shook the ants from her dark wings.

"That you even have to ask shows how much damage the curse has done to you. Tell me, had you ever done that when you were in your human skin?"

Shaking her head, the crow answered, "I don't suppose so."

"You're more trouble than you're worth," he seethed as his warm breath met the air, and a cloud of steam rose before his face.

"I ensured all the ants stayed perched upon my wings and out of your precious kitchen," the crow huffed, shaking the insects from her feathers. "That's three times I've helped you only to earn your ire. *You're* more trouble than *you're* worth!"

"Pah!" Crevan seethed. "You're a supercilious little monster."

The crow cawed, turning her back on him. "And you're a grumpy toad eater."

"Well, this *toad eater* just cured one of your ailments. Perhaps you're too good to eat my fare which would transform you to your normal self. If that's the case, I shall wash my hands of you at once. Good day, Lady Crow." Crevan turned on his booted heel and proceeded to stride away. He wouldn't suffer abuse from an insignificant being.

"Wait," she cried out.

Crevan halted his steps but refused to turn back toward her. *Let her beg for my help.* Tingles tiptoed over his skin and along his scalp at his ungracious thought.

"I am very much in need of your assistance. I would be happy to be *indebted* to you for whatever length you feel is necessary," her voice warbled, and Crevan heard the flutter of wings taking flight.

"Hmmm," he stroked his chin mentally calculating all the potential ways this could possibly backfire on him. True, she was a bother and he didn't like other beings in his space. Was she a being that could be trusted? The timing was impeccable, and he needed assistance. Slowly, Crevan nodded his head.

"Any length of time? Well, that is convenient for me. Come along, let's not dally any longer." His body was beginning to chill from the frosty temperature. He began making his way to his cottage and left it up to her to decide whether she wanted to accept his offer. Crevan wasn't in the habit of forcing others, and certainly not *mortals,* into his company.

Chapter Four

Bare Legs?

The door shut firmly behind Arabella, and she took a moment to wonder whether obtaining Grumpy's aid was a good idea or would only lead to more trouble for her. She craved being human again, but being a crow had made it easier to fill her stomach. Her difficulties seemed easier to manage in a bird body. But if she were to stay here in the safety of the shoppe, perhaps her life might change direction, and she would be alright. Grumpy was prickly, but he hadn't been cruel to her, not unjustly so.

She flew silently behind the faerie as they once again found themselves in the kitchen. Arabella perched atop the counter and peered closely over to the napkin. Her curse breaker impatiently waved his hand over the chocolate cake and mint macaroon.

"If you would be so kind as to take a few bites. I do have some accounting to see to in my office before the next day dawns." He sniffed and folded his arms over his tidy tailcoat.

Hopping over to the sweets, Arabella took a deep breath and made a wish that someday she'd find her place in the world. Her beak delicately bit into a thick layer of chocolate icing, and she moaned as the decadent flavor exploded on her tongue. After swallowing that bite, she bent forward and pecked at the moist cake, taking a beakful and savoring the moment. Had she ever tasted anything so exquisite before?

"Now the macaroon," Grumpy instructed as his eyes narrowed at her. He seemed to be studying her. Did he doubt his creation's ability to break the enchantment?

Arabella's tiny bird feet moved her to the macaroon, and she licked the top of it. Liquid lightning burst through her body, her breaths became labored, and a bright light robbed her of sight. Arabella wanted to scream from the agony, but only a quiet hiss escaped her mouth as her legs wobbled and she fell into a black abyss.

"I say, are you quite well now?" Grumpy asked as he leaned over her, his warm breath tickling the shell of her ear.

An ear? Gingerly, Arabella raised her arm to her head, covering her ear with her palm. A rush of exhilaration soared through her heart, and tears pricked her eyes. Human, she was herself again.

"Mute? Did the hex malfunction?" Dark brows furrowed as the fae scowled.

"Nnn...oooo—," she stuttered.

"Ah, very good. Well, we can't have your indecent body lingering on my kitchen tiles any longer."

Arabella nearly shrieked when she looked down her body to the bare legs that his pristine black tailcoat hid. *Naked!* She was completely bare beneath the scratchy fabric of his coat. Arabella's stomach knotted and her heart skipped a beat. She hung her head, allowing her dark tresses to cover her face and hang over her shoulders.

How utterly mortifying!

"Help me?" she croaked. Her mouth was bone dry, and her tongue was sandpaper in her mouth as she attempted to swallow.

"As you wish," he replied, rising, then offering his hand for her to take. Arabella reached out her arm along the opening of the lapels, her hand hesitating for a moment before grasping the faerie's hand. Warmth traveled from the tips of his fingers to hers, along her arm, and straight into the center of her heart.

When he pulled her to her feet, they stood toe-to-toe, amber and emerald gazes locked in a trance. Good heavens, what was happening? Arabella wanted to simultaneously cling to him and throw herself backward to avoid him. The atmosphere was charged like a rushing current, and she felt helpless in its flow.

The faerie cleared his throat and slowly withdrew his hand, allowing Arabella's hand to drop to her side. He seemed to be warring with himself as he stepped away from her. His body was bent toward her at an odd angle as he fumbled.

"You can have my sofa tonight. We'll work on a more permanent solution tomorrow. I'd offer you more privacy, but it isn't to be found here. I only have an office. I take my meals at my desk and find my rest on my sofa. If you can refrain from making a—"

"A mess? Yes, I know by now that you do like your things orderly," Arabella interrupted his speech while she tried to gather his tailcoat more securely to her. Switching her eyes downward, she asked, "You didn't stare, right?" At his perplexed look, she added, "When I was *naked.*"

Grumpy straightened to his full height and looked down at her with widened eyes. "What kind of a faerie do you take me for?"

"Well, I don't really know you, and the fae are experts at trickery. You didn't, did you?" Arabella's pale toes curled as she inwardly cringed.

His resounding "*No!*" was like a cannon shot, reverberating against the walnut walls and rattling the marzipan windows.

"Thank—," she paused, remembering the fae hated politeness. "That's quite wonderful."

"I shall try to find you decent attire," he replied, swiveling on his booted heel and striding toward his office.

Crevan's mind was foggy in his haste to distance himself from the most beautiful creature he had ever seen. Her alluring scent of honeysuckle and cinnamon clung in the air, chasing after him like some spectral ghost. As he left the kitchen, he grumbled under his breath, striding with a purposeful gait to the furthest side wall and the hidden doorway.

With a wave toward the area where a handle would be, swirling golden stars shimmered, and the door opened itself. Crevan walked in and made his way to the chests that lined the wall beneath an enchanted large bay window. The window wasn't real but had been spelled to keep perfect time with the outside world.

He huffed out a breath. The last thing a faerie wanted was to have others nosing into their business. Crevan stopped at the first chest, bending forward to release the latch, he flipped open the lid and rummaged through the contents. He cheered silently as he located clothing that might cover her and keep all the creamy skin from his eyes. It wasn't his fault that his gaze had landed on her legs, and though he was a gentle-faerie, he had had to look at her just the teeniest bit when he caught her. She had been pliant and soft in his arms, the perfect vision to a faerie who had sworn off the charms of the fairer ladyfolk. He had his priorities, after all, his confectionery being his life's work. Romance, whether for a night or a lifetime, was *not* in his future.

Straightening to his full height, Crevan ran a hand over his face and sighed. He would be a ruined fool if he let any creature dwell within his heart or mind. He shuddered as an icy chill danced over his spine. He had almost kissed the vixen! Had he not pulled himself away from her intoxicating warmth, he very likely would have pressed his lips to hers. He, the most determined male in either realm, always managed to rein in his emotions and *always* keep a safe distance. What had come over him? Hardening his mouth in a fierce frown and turning his eyes to slits, he exited his office. He was ready to do battle, the most important battle of his life, if the prickling of his heart was any indication.

Chapter Five

Grumpy Trousers Has A Name

Arabella covered her flaming cheeks with her hands, wishing she could briefly turn back into a bird and fly away to save herself from the entire embarrassing predicament. How could she be drawn to the cantankerous being? And what had possessed her to almost allow him to kiss her? Where had her morals fled to? If the male fae wasn't so abhorrently curt, she might go so far as considering him quite attractive, with his amber eyes and tawny silky hair.

What mess have I found myself in now? If I didn't get his help, I would, perchance, forever be stuck as a bird, and now that I've gotten his help, I'm stuck again.

Arabella lowered her hands, then pulled the coat tighter around herself.

"Here," he said, voice booming as he loomed over her. She must have been woolgathering to not have noticed his return. "Dress yourself," he continued as he thrust a bundle of fabric toward her.

Taking the bundle from his outstretched hand, Arabella held the clothes close to her chest. "Where?"

He groaned, grabbing her elbow, and pulled her along from the kitchen toward his office door. When he waved his hand, waking the magical spell, the door sprang open, and he let go of her arm as if touching her was a torment.

"Better?" he bit out as his lips twisted into a sneer.

Arabella nodded her head, but she flinched when he slammed the door, leaving her alone in his personal space. She wanted to spy on what treasures he kept in the secret chamber, to discover what it was that he prized. But she didn't dare keep him waiting.

She quickly padded to the large ornate desk and set the clothing atop it. Picking up a pair of navy breeches, much too long for her, she swiftly stepped into them, pulling them on. Next, Arabella unfolded a matching navy shirt that was much too long, hanging to mid-thigh and well over her hands. She was able to wrest the fabric over her wrists by folding it several times. Lastly, gathering the loose neckline into a knot, she was as decent as she could be. At least she wouldn't be in danger of showing too much skin.

Arabella swiped her raven curls out of her face and wished for hair pins or a ribbon to secure the unruly tresses. Bending down, she rolled up the extra length of fabric from each trouser leg. The last thing she needed was to trip and be an even bigger burden to the surly fae, whose name she didn't even know. She couldn't very well continue to address him as *Grumpy Trousers.* He was certain to be offended by that. Advancing back to the room's door, Arabella took a deep breath and exhaled it as she tried to still the racing of her heart. The blood was rushing through her veins with the force of an untamed river.

"I'm decent," she yelled once she felt that she had gained her composure.

The door swung inward, and there he was. He came striding forward; dark brows pulled low over his keen amber eyes. His tail twitched behind him, matching his crossed arms and the tapping fingers, alluding to his displeasure. Would he always be so vexed at her?

Arabella peered around him. "Are you a squirrel?"

Grumpy perked a brow. "Heavens, NO!"

"So, what are you?"

"Currently, irate—"

"What else is new? But my question was, what species are you?"

Grumpy strode past her and further into his office. "Go to bed," he muttered.

Rounding on him, she replied, "You're the one who needs sleep. Are you always this prickly?"

"And more," he growled, pointing toward the emerald sofa that rested near the dark fireplace.

Crossing her arms over her chest, Arabella's tone was icy as she said, "My name is Arabella. What's yours?"

"I'm Crevan, not that *that's* important to you. Now, off you go to Slumberland!"

"What type of shifter are you, Crevan? Perhaps something embarrassing?" Her eyes narrowed as she snapped her fingers and tilted her head. "A weasel then?"

"Why all the incessant questions?"

"Answer this one, and I'll stop. If you're not a weasel or a squirrel, then what are you?"

"I'm a fox! Now, before I change my mind and turn you back, go to bed!" he fumed at her, and she was mildly surprised that steam wasn't coming from his ears—he looked ready to boil over.

"I'm going, *Crevan,*" she conceded, heading to the sofa. A fox? It suited him, for she imagined that he could be sneaky and even stealthy when the occasion called for it.

"Can you be quiet while I work?"

"Like the dead," she sarcastically replied, sitting on the cushy dark sofa.

He smirked, taking a seat in his dark leather office chair. He strummed his fingers on the desktop, staring at her. "I'm curious," he began, picking up a quill pen. "What made you steal the king's prized fruit?"

"I didn't know they were strictly for him. Some fae in a hooded cloak told me if I ate it, my deepest desire would be granted."

"That's extremely selfish of you."

"So selfish to want a home?"

"You wanted a home? Of all the things you wasted a magic berry on, it was a home?"

"It means everything to someone who doesn't have one," she replied, her voice cracking as self-loathing made her chest squeeze painfully. "I was apprehended before I could even wish for it."

Crevan nodded. "Well, good thing it didn't go to waste then. For you've found a home of sorts, at least for the time being."

"I suppose so. At least until you tire of me."

"Do the humans you consort with often find you tiresome?" he asked as he studied her.

"I wouldn't know what they think of me. It's not as if I can ask them," she paused as her lips dipped into a frown. "Do you go around inquiring what others think of you?"

"Dear heavens, no! How *unfaely* to worry over such a trivial matter."

"You haven't ever cared what opinions you garner from others?" It shouldn't surprise her. Not when he was so brusk with her. Though, there was a tiny part of her that cared about what *he* thought of her.

"There are no opinions that matter much to me. I am who I am."

"But—" Arabella couldn't halt her tongue from spilling the question tumbling around in her mind. "Do you have no sweetheart? No lady fae who makes your heart flutter or feel as if you were as light as a feather?"

"That sounds ghastly. No, I have never been so besotted. The idea doesn't even seem worth entertaining," said Crevan as a muscle in his cheek ticked. A slight blush infused his face as he swiftly cast his eyes away from her.

Arabella's mind was churning when the sound of his voice made her jump.

"You haven't ever been so enamored of a fellow before have you? No silly suitor waiting at home for you?"

"For me?" She had to bring her hand up to cover her mouth to stifle the giggle that wanted to peal into the air. Arabella removed her hand, masking her emotions with a serious facade. Why not pretend? It would be so easy where Crevan was concerned. "Tons of beaus. They practically line up. I'm up to my neck in bouquets and the best French smelling perfumes. The gifts are endless as is the praise. They write me sonnets."

"Sonnets?" Crevan's face soured on the word.

"Sheets and sheets." The giggle finally broke free and it reverberated around the office.

Crevan pointed a finger at her before replying, "You are quite the storyteller. Shall we be adding that to the list of your best traits?"

"Are you cataloging my best traits?" Surprise shot from her toes to the tip of her head.

Clearing his throat, Crevan said, "If such a list were being created, that might be a plus for a human, who needs to be crafty enough to survive here in Faerie."

"Oh, of course." Was she disappointed or not? Why did her heart soar with the idea that she might be of interest to him as more than just a pest.

"Best to take your rest. The morrow shall be here in practically no time at all." Crevan moved his eyes from her to scan the contents atop his desk. "And soon, I shall be collecting on your debt. You may yet find a home of your own with— " His fist rubbed the area over his heart.

"With?" she prompted.

"Some mortal who you may deserve, safely tucked away on the human side of The Wall. That is what you wish? To return home? To make a home of your own?" Looking up, his eyes roved over her face and she wondered what flaws he was discovering, even more so than when she had been naked in his kitchen.

"It is."

"See that you steer clear of conniving faeries and absurd wishes," his tone grew harsh and she felt soundly dismissed as he opened a ledger and began to peruse the cream parchment.

Settling her head down on one of the plush pillows, Arabella reached for the wool blanket hanging on the back of the sofa, shaking it before she allowed it to fall over her body. While she could easily argue with him about how she came to be in this land until she was blue in the face, there really was little use in the matter. He was a faerie, and the fae were convinced of their superiority in every situation.

Closing her eyes, she idly thought about her treasure in the abandoned nest. Should she even attempt to return her stolen goods or just let them be? Arabella could only imagine the trouble she would bring to herself and now also to Crevan. She was certain he would throw her out into the snow should she prove to be more of a handful.

So, even though she hated the idea of obeying him, it was best that she attempted to please him, if only for a little while. As Arabella drifted off, it was to happy thoughts of a home of her own.

Chapter Six

Fluffy Tail

From dreaming about a windswept meadow where the flowers bobbed along the breeze, Arabella was catapulted to wakefulness by a little fellow insistently poking her side. Just managing to stifle her scream, she sucked in air and began to cough. The little dwarf tugged her upright and thumped upon her back. Arabella gathered herself and waved him away with the flick of her hand.

"I'm perfectly fine now," she said, looking beyond the magenta hat in search of Crevan. What time was it, and where was he?

Rubbing the sleep from her eyes, Arabella threw the blanket aside and stood. Wrinkles and creases lined her borrowed clothing, and if the tangled knots in the hair hanging over her shoulder were any indication, she looked afright. How would she manage to be useful to her host if her clothing made her look like a vagabond?

Arabella felt tugging on her trousers which brought her attention back to the dwarf. The little being was looking up at her with an adoring look. He was holding aloft before her a package wrapped in brown paper and tied with a string.

"For me?" she questioned as she demurely smiled down at him.

He nodded, the skin around his eyes pinching together as his smile widened.

Sitting back down, Arabella laid the gift onto her lap and pulled the string free. She gently unwrapped the paper and gasped as warmth enveloped her heart and moisture pooled in her eyes. There, in the contents of the paper, was a periwinkle empire-waisted dress with delicate snowflakes sewn onto it.

The dwarf reached up to cup her cheek and shook his head as his pale blue eyes clouded with uncertainty.

Clearing her throat, she rushed to say, "This is for me? I can hardly remember the last time I was given a gift, and this is...it's quite stunning. I love it."

Twirling on his feet in a happy dance, her gift-giver clapped his hands. Then he motioned to her to look under the dress. When Arabella did so, she spied undergarments, making her face heat up as a blush crept over it. Her fingers fumbled to uncover a set of matching silk slippers. Again, she had to collect her feelings and lock them away into a box; if she began to cry over the attire, she may never be able to stem her tears.

Pushing to her feet, she hugged the things to her chest and beamed down at her friend, for he was a friend, and for a moment, she wondered if she had ever really had a friend before. Perchance, this was another first for her here in Faerie.

"I'm only an ordinary human girl; this is much too fine for me. It's better suited to a princess—"

Insistently shaking his dark head and narrowing his eyes, he shook his finger at her in admonishment. Then he mimicked threading a needle and sewing motions.

"You made this for me?" Arabella's brows drew together.

When he nodded, she could no longer contain her tears, and one slipped down her face. "I'm only mortal," she began and proceeded only when she knew he was listening carefully. "And we humans do like to express our gratitude when one makes us happier than we've ever been. So I thank you most sincerely."

The dwarf's eyes lit with cheer as his cocoa skin took on a rosy shade.

It was days like these that Crevan wished he had a waitstaff to help with the hustle and bustle. He was up to the pointed tips of his ears in tables that needed to be cleared and treats that needed to be restocked. Not to mention the buzzing noise of his patrons, who were all excitedly discussing the latest village gossip about some silly goose marrying a turtle. Of all the perplexing shifter marriages, *that* was one for the history tomes.

The rustling of silk and muslin caught his attention, and he looked up from the counter. He nearly choked on his own spittle when his eyes landed on Arabella. Donned in a soft blue day dress, she looked spectacular. His heart began to furiously thump in his chest as he sought to blink and swallow to moisten his mouth. Her creamy complexion was fairly aglow under the floating fae lights, and her wild curls had been tamed; they still cascaded down her back and hugged her shoulders, but with the heavy mass framing her heart-shaped face, she was...ethereal. A goddess. How was he to perform his duties when he couldn't look away from her? This was the worst idea ever. *She* was the worst idea ever. But here she was, and he needed her assistance. His mind urged him to send her away, but his heart begged him to allow her to stay. It was quite the conundrum.

"Do I measure up?" Her timid voice rescued him from his inner musings.

"Indeed. Have a bit of whatever catches your eye. Then perhaps you can help to clear the tables?"

"Absolutely, I am yours to direct," she said as she glided around the counter's end and peered into the display glass.

The frigid morning air swept through the confectionery, biting exposed flesh as a trio of the king's guards came through the entrance. Crevan rushed to grab menus and dashed over to greet them. He passed Arabella as she brought over hot chocolates for the customers to warm up with and savor, but each time he passed her, he had to train his eyes not to wander back to her beauty. As they made their way through each task the hectic morning soon gave way to a more sedate afternoon.

In the kitchen, Arabella was gathering clean dishes from the sink. Coming up behind her, he leaned against the counter to face her.

"How do you feel about Valentine's Day?" he asked as a tart taste filled his mouth.

"I don't feel strongly about it either way. Why do you ask?"

"The king has requested that we celebrate the human holiday. It's ridiculous, and I don't want to. But even I can't go against his wishes; I wouldn't dare." Crevan hunched his shoulders.

"Celebrate how?" she asked, arching her brows.

"We are to decorate and make our clientele feel warm and fuzzy, not with my confections alone, but with the atmosphere. So I ask you, have you any idea how to go about this? Do I need to fashion a heart-shaped fountain? Cut out bows and arrows or doves? I could perhaps concoct a brew that makes one feel in love, a special love potion as it were, but the last time I did so and freely handed it out, every faerie was kissing every faerie, and I had to lock myself in my office to avoid several amorous winged fae. I don't relish the memory, and I dread the idea of creating new ones." A full-bodied shudder made goosebumps form along his arms under his clothing.

Arabella covered her mouth with her hand, but Crevan still saw the secret smile. He wondered if he could bring a full-fledged smile upon her lips, one that would brighten her eyes.

"I assure you, it wasn't a humorous event."

Removing her hand, she allowed her smile to show, and the full force of it directed at him made his breath catch in his throat, and his heart skip a beat. Crevan felt a hint of fear steal into his being, with its icy fingers coasting along his skin. He wanted to flee but was overcome with an even bigger realization that he wanted to bask in her presence. What was happening to him?

"Of course not. It's only that the thought of you cowering in a corner just seems to delight my senses and tickle my soul," she replied with apparent glee, lighting up her emerald eyes with a sparkle he had never witnessed from her before.

Clearing his throat, Crevan glared at her, if only to remind himself that she wasn't his friend. When she didn't seem to mind his ire, he said, "Would you for once answer my question? Can you manage to decorate or work some human charm to help my shoppe for this insipid Valentine's Day?"

"I can, and I will happily see to the task. Only, I find that my mind is thoroughly distracted, and I am not certain whether I can accomplish all that you need unless..."

"Go on," he ordered her with a wave of his hand.

"Would you mind showing me your fox form? Now, before you go shouting and threatening me, consider the fact that I have *endless* questions, and I am not currently plaguing you with them. I only ask for one teeny little peep. Of course, I could commence with my *million and one* questions, such as how tiny are you when you are in your Unseelie form? Is your coat shiny? Do your teeth—"

"Enough!" Crevan bellowed as his face mottled to a stained cherry hue. Looking away from her, he scanned the area. Seeing that all his customers were happily situated, he crooked his finger at her, beckoning her to follow after him. Turning, he marched to his office door, used his magic to open it, ushered her inside, and softly shut the door after her.

"Watch closely, as I will only do this *once*. I haven't the time to indulge you again. Have you any idea what a nightmare fox hair is to remove from one's clothing? Stand close, but do not touch." Rolling his eyes, he inhaled deeply, then felt the well of magic he cradled in his core expand as its warmth traveled the length of his limbs. With a shimmery golden hue that emanated from him like the gentle rays of the dawning day, a shrinking sensation made his stomach flutter, and he landed upon four feet. Shaking his head, Crevan felt his fur stand on end before resting against his body. He waited for the woman to say something, to pass some judgment onto him that he wasn't certain he wanted to hear. Was he pleasing to her? While in this form before, he had never had a reason to question whether he was beautiful. He knew deep in his soul that his fox half was glorious; he was a perfect specimen, and yet... He felt his insides seize up at the idea that she might find him lacking, unworthy of her praise.

"You are such a pretty boy!" she cooed as she bent down to better observe him. When she reached out a hand to hang in the air above his head, waiting for his assent or denial before her fingers tangled in his fur, Crevan ducked his head in submission.

Arabella didn't waste a moment, the tips of her fingers grazed against his skin as they separated his fur in long trails. The soft touches, the caresses, made his eyes close, and he had to lock his jaw to keep his traitorous tongue from peeking from his mouth to limply hang over his teeth in a delighted manner. Could she really be his mate? The one being in all the world created just for him? Was it so preposterous an idea? She had borne his foul humor, had stood toe-to-toe with him, and still, she hadn't broken or run screaming from his side. Mortals never knew the havoc a Fated Mate could wreck on one's entire world. They simply weren't made for housing a bond until their other half presented it to them. Nurtured the tether and accepted it wholeheartedly. Could he do those things? Did he even want to try?

His thoughts went back to the evening before. She had been so...what was the word? And her beautiful face had been so peaceful while she slumbered. Crevan had felt like the worst deviant whenever he caught his eyes drifting over her blanketed-form. It had been a monumental feat to train his eyes away and to the task of tracking his expenses.

Arabella's gentle hands wound their way down his back and along his tail, which was standing at attention.

"You've such a fluffy tail in either state. It's truly adorable."

Adorable? He snorted. It was his most masculine trait while on four feet! Was he upset, or was that pride swirling in his stomach like the delicate, satiny wings of a butterfly?

Jerking away from her, Crevan drew on his powers and transformed back to his Seelie self within mere seconds. Before the golden light of his shift had faded, he was stalking toward the door and striding through it. Canting his head over his shoulder, he said, "Do use the bristled brush in the top drawer of my desk to remove any lingering hair. In the middle drawer, you will find shears and thread, lace, and odd bits of material. See what your imagination can fathom for this stupid holiday."

"Do you not believe in love?" He caught her softly spoken question and halted his steps outside the doorway.

Crevan didn't turn to face her; how could he? She was the embodiment of this ridiculous holiday. Perhaps she was his perfect mate, but he wasn't sure that she would even want to stay in Faerie with him. Could his heart survive her abandonment? Even worse, would his goods suffer the same fate as his broken heart?

"I don't believe in celebrating some obtuse holiday to find love. One day, to treat your other half like royalty, to stuff them with sweets, and to recite horrid poetry that isn't even your own. What rubbish and a complete waste."

"But do you find that some can't express their feelings easily, and they rely on the help of the day to inspire them to greater passions?" Her voice was like the softest velvet assaulting his senses.

"More fools them," he snapped as he walked away.

Chapter Seven

A Ridiculous Holiday

Was it a ridiculous holiday? When put into the words that Crevan had used, it certainly seemed so. And though she had never celebrated it before, this year, Arabella was thrilled with the idea of filling the entire confectionery with all the ooey-gooey lovey-dovey things that others seemed to adore. The mental image of her host, her employer, standing amid hearts was just too good to deny. Arabella had to make her vision come to life. He would look magnificent as the focal point of her decorating, with his amber eyes glowering at her and his auburn hair gleaming in the low lighting. The portrait in her mind of the striking appearance he always cut with his immaculate manner of attire robbed the breath from her body. *Good Heavens!* She was more than a little attracted to him, which spelled utter disaster since she was not fae. Best to put such odd notions far from her mind.

Sitting down in the leather chair before the desk, Arabella took a moment to breathe. She wasn't being hunted, wasn't in danger of starving, didn't have to scout out a safer area to find rest in, and wasn't in need of a bath. In a sense, though she was bound to Crevan in word, she had never felt quite so free. Even in crow form, she had not been her own master. The treasures she had amassed made her a slave who could never be content with all the bits and bobbles overflowing in her nest. If she never set eyes on her foul home or its contents again, she would be very happy.

Enough dilly-dallying; it was time to see what she could create from what lay in the fox shifter's desk. The first drawer held bundles of cream parchment, and to the side was the brush she had been ordered to use. Withdrawing a handful of parchment sheets, she gently set them to rest on the desktop and then closed the drawer. She didn't feel like wasting time brushing her dress free from any errant fur. In the long, slim drawer that spanned the middle width of the desk, Arabella located the golden shears and laid them atop the parchment. Riffling through the rulers and the bits of ribbons and twine, Arabella's lips curved into a grin. Hearts! She could fashion hearts from the paper and use the white and red ribbons to hang the hearts from. She'd rather have found a way to make the cream parchment a pale shade of peach or vibrant red; even a light pink would do. But she had nothing to use to give color to them. If only Crevan shared his creative genius with watercolors, then she could paint them. Dare she ask for paints? There probably wasn't time to procure them and have the shoppe decorated in time.

Looking to the side wall where the mahogany bookshelves stood, Arabella spied a scarlet beeswax candle that had been burned before but still had a long way to go before it was spent. Biting her bottom lip, she looked to the door and back to the shelf. In England, beeswax was found only in the very upper crust of Society, and she had only seen one beeswax candle when a lady had entreated her to help a footman carry her many packages to her residence in Mayfair. Would Crevan be upset if she used the littlest amount of wax just to outline some of the hearts? He had said to make use of his things...

Gingerly, Arabella rose and padded over toward the candle. With tentative fingers, she reached up to pluck the candle from the shelf and moved her gaze to the fireplace. Could she use a stick to light her flame? Once she stood before the fire grate, Arabella bent and picked through the wicker basket housing the tinder. Locating a tiny branch, she held it toward the blue flame and watched the tip alight. A rush of excitement made her cheeks flush, and a squeal left her mouth. Tossing the branch into the flickering flames, she walked back to the desk and held the burning candle at an angle to drip over several sheets of paper. She traced four hearts on each piece of parchment, and when she was done, the candle was no shorter, nor was the wick in need of trimming. Drawing her brows together and tilting her head, Arabella shrugged her shoulders and blew the flame out. Wisps of white smoke plumed before her face, and Arabella made a wish that she could stay in Crevan's good graces and please him with a job well done.

Taking her seat, Arabella set the candle down and picked up the shears to begin cutting out the hearts.

Higglehugh held the wooden ladder's base as Arabella swiftly climbed. The vaulted ceiling was beautiful, but it was difficult to reach the beams. And she envisioned letting the hearts dangle down in vertical columns, suspended just above the floating faerie lights. They were attached to red ribbons in lines of five. She trusted the little dwarf to keep the ladder steady as he had been so pleasant to her, assisting her with locating the ladder from a supply closet. It was just past closing, and Crevan had raised his dark brows as she and Higglehugh carried the ladder between them. From over his shoulder, Crevan cautioned the dwarf by name, and now, Arabella was delighted to have something to call her helper. With her employer locked in his office, it was time for the dwarfs to tidy the establishment. They hummed a merry tune as they worked, and their medley lit a soft glow in Arabella's heart. Every so often, she descended the ladder's steps to move it a few feet away and begin the process of hanging hearts. Once the last ribbon was hung, she stood back to examine her work. It was an excellent start.

"Higglehugh," she turned to address her companion. "Do you know where we can gather some flowers? I realize it's wintertide, but perhaps some hothouse exists that we may take from?"

With a nod of his head, the serious little being grabbed her hand and drew her toward the exit. He stopped and clicked his fingers together. From the ether, a dark velvet cloak appeared, and he moved it to her. Arabella drew the material over her as another click of his fingers produced a similar cloak for him. When they were both properly attired to face the frosty evening, he twisted the lock and pulled the door open. Outside, a flurry of falling snow glinting in the moonlight gave the appearance of glittering diamonds. With frosty breaths leaving steaming puffs before the pair, they trekked over the paver stones, and the crunch of ice broke the peaceful setting. Following on the dwarf's heels, Arabella watched her steps, taking care not to slip.

With only the teal moonlight to shine a glow down upon them, Arabella's eyes felt weak in the dim lighting, but she trusted her friend.

They continued along in the opposite direction of Crevan's secret atrium. Just when Arabella felt that it might be better to give up the endeavor altogether, she began to see the tops of chimneys chugging smoke into the night air through the knotted fingers of barren tree branches and limbs that eerily rose toward the sky.

A stone pathway presented itself, and Higglehugh stepped onto it, certain of their direction. The pathway led the pair along a winding passage, and soon, they were surrounded by houses with thatched roofs. Icicles clung all along the outside of the adorable homes, and quaint little yards were dotted with delightful snowfae standing as silent sentinels facing the cobblestone road. The snow creatures were charming with their coal eyes, knitted scarves, and a variety of head-wear; the gleaming top hats and bonnets collected snowflakes that glittered like spun sugar crystals.

Pivoting back to Arabella, the dwarf again excitedly took hold of her gloveless hand and guided her past the homes with their frosted windows and down toward what seemed to be the very center of the village. There was a circular glass dome over a patch of greenery, and as they drew nearer, Arabella was able to spy the different colored petals of a plethora of flowers. The breath in her chest halted. She bunched her shoulders and wrinkled her nose, and a surge of eagerness had her rushing forward. Higglehugh released her hand, and his tiny legs propelled him past her and through the enclosure. It shimmered with blue and purple light as his body passed through it, and Arabella didn't waste a moment in following after him. When she was crossing by, a tingling sensation began in her toes and worked its way up to her head, and the tiny hairs along her arms rose. The phenomena lasted only a few moments but it left Arabella feeling refreshed. She suppressed the giggle that nearly broke free.

"How glorious!" she exclaimed.

Before them were roses in shades of pink, red, purple, white, and yellow. Further scanning the blooms, Arabella cataloged peonies, sweet peas, lilies, and delphinium. She even spotted some exotic flowers such as dahlias, nerines, and fuschia growing in beautiful symmetry surrounding a small rock pond that koi goldfish happily swam in. Above their heads, golden lanterns with rippling blue flames hung suspended in the air. In the very midst of wintertide, this was an unexpected delight that warmed her heart.

Pursing her lips, she debated whether it was safe to take a few flowers. "Higglehugh, are you certain that we may take these?" The last thing she desired was a repeat of being accused of stealing.

The dwarf vigorously nodded his head and bent forward, plucking a peony from its stem. Before their very eyes, another flower began to bud and bloom, and within another few heartbeats, the new flower stood as tall as its fellows.

"Oh, it's enchanted! How marvelous! Let's be quick about it and return before we're missed. I can't wait to see the shoppe decked out with a riot of color and the aroma of fresh blossoms floating in every corner and crevice." The very thought brought a beaming smile to her face.

Chapter Eight

Icky Lickers

An odd wailing sound drew Crevan from his account books and immediately put him into a surly mood. With lightning-quick footsteps, he left his office behind and strode to the very center of his establishment. Turning his head to the side, he let his ears hone in on the sound, which came again with renewed vigor.

Before he could take a step toward the wall nearest the counter, the front door crashed open, setting the bell above the door to clanging, and a bevy of swirling snowflakes flew into his shoppe as Higglehugh and Arabella entered. Their arms were laden down with greenery, and glee seemed to dance along the excited woman's facade as a puddle of slush surrounded her booted feet. Her eyes shone with deep wells of happiness and her face was glowing, and not just from the pink hue caused by being out in the cold. Was this a normal occurrence for her? He rubbed a hand over his aching chest and frowned, wondering why he was bothered that she had found such joy in being removed from his presence.

"Oh, Crevan, do be a dear and help me, won't you?" Arabella called out to him with a brilliance in her tone that made him think of rose-golden sun rays.

Without thinking, he closed the distance and allowed her to pile his arms with blooms. Inhaling the confusing scent of many flowers made his nose itch, and he sneezed.

"Oh goodness, I hope you aren't allergic," she said as her smile morphed into a concerned frown. She brought the back of her smooth hand to rest against his forehead. "Hmmm..."

Pulling away as if her touch had scorched him, he grimaced and said, "I am quite well. Fae never become ill—"

A sob interrupted his words, and Crevan turned his head toward the glass counter, then back to Arabella when she gasped.

Bringing her hands up to the sides of her face, Arabella's enlarged eyes searched his, and he narrowed his gaze at her.

"What is that?" she asked in a voice brimming with accusation.

Crevan huffed before replying, "How should I know?" Switching his gaze to Higglehugh, he addressed him. "Go see what exactly that noise is stemming from."

Higglehugh's brows furrowed as he shook his head and juggled his arms. The heads of the blossoms shook at Crevan with a surprising amount of stamina, given the fact that they were dead and decaying.

Crevan rolled his eyes and marched over to the counter display, taking care not to crush even a single petal, and carefully laid the flora down. He heard the swish of Arabella's dress as she came up behind him. Higglehugh busied himself with his armload, dispersing them atop one of the wooden table tops. Crevan rounded the counter and entered through the side entrance; he cautiously peered at the walnut wall to the side of the counter.

"Oh, for all the realm's sake. An icky licker!" he said, his face twisting into a sneer.

"A what?" Arabella asked as she speedily made her way to his side.

"You know, this is all *your* fault," he accused as he pinched the bridge of his nose.

"Whatever can you mean? My fault, indeed? But...," she responded, creeping closer to the wall. "What exactly is my fault?"

Crevan watched her brows raise, and her mouth form a perfect "*o*" before she raced to the wall and the little faerieling that was currently attached to it. Kneeling beside him, she patted his back and made cooing noises to him, which only served to make the little one wail with more force as his limbs failed. Arabella had to duck one of his flying fists.

"Do something!" she cried.

"Why should I? I wasn't the one to steal into my confectionery and lick the wall. Why, he's receiving the punishment he deserves." Crevan looked on with mild interest at the portly little body. He was fairly certain that the young one's girth wasn't due to Crevan's confections. There was a distinct difference between natural weight, which weighed one down, and magical mass, which lent a certain buoyancy to one. This faerieling enjoyed a good appetite. It was no wonder that his tongue was stuck to the wall.

"That is terrible! Do you want him gone? Rescue him." Arabella clasped onto the creature's chin and gave it an experimental tug, which made the tan tail sticking out from the seam of the faerie's trousers wave with a frantic tempo.

Sighing heavily, Crevan wheeled on his booted heel and returned to the glass counter. *Why am I doomed to never enjoy a moment's peace?* Sliding the glass to the side, his fingers reached in and withdrew a single chocolate-frosted fig. He retraced his steps and handed the fig to Arabella. Taking it, she examined it, twisting it around in the palm of her hand.

"How does he eat it when his tongue is affixed to the wall?"

"Rub it along his tongue," Crevan explained as his thinning patience stretched. He wasn't annoyed at her, not really. Still, if she had locked the door, they wouldn't be in this situation. Trouble seemed to follow in her wake. He was always up for entertainment and liked the effects his sweets had on others, but only during normal business hours. Every faerie had his limits.

Arabella moved the fig to the faerieling's tongue, and her brow wrinkled as drool began to drip from the boy's open mouth. The chocolate goo trailed down his chin and straight to his shirt as he began to glow a deep purple. A pop sounded, and the little fae fell backward against Arabella's lap.

Scrambling to encircle the creature, fearing it would attach itself back to the wall, Arabella's lithe arms attempted to keep the faerieling against her. But as the little one wriggled against her, she realized that she was about to let it go. It was just too strong for her to subdue.

"Higglehugh," she grunted under the fae's weight, "could you pl—," she stopped, grunting as the lizard-like creature fought against her. "Would you mind getting the door?"

Higglehugh gave a gruff nod, trotting over to the door. Arabella huffed and grunted, using all her might, she rose and began to tug the portly creature over to the door. The faerieling's tongue lapped at the air and lassoed around its head. Arabella screeched at the wicked and wiley tongue as it almost made contact with her face.

"Oh no," she muttered, yanking the creature further toward the door, "you don't! Keep that tongue in your mouth!"

The faerieling thrashed against her body, attempting to free itself of her vice-like grasp. Why had she ever allowed herself to feel one moment's sorrow for the sad state they had found it in? The being was repulsive! Arabella was on the threshold of the door. With a final shove, she threw the creature out and slammed the door shut; the bell above them merrily chimed away. Higglehugh locked the door at the base while she got the other lock at the top. There was no way she was allowing the fat faerie into the shoppe ever again, even if he returned with coins bulging from his pockets.

Collecting her breath, she glanced over her shoulder at Crevan, who had a hand pressed over his mouth. "What?"

"You could have just asked it to leave and given it the candied fig," he said nonchalantly with a shrug of one shoulder.

Arabella scowled at him, stomping her way back to the flowers as she used all of her willpower to gain a modicum of poise. She leaned up against the counter, fiddling through the gathered bunches until she found a yellow rose. Gently, Arabella plucked it and held it out to him.

"Here's this flower, now, could you *please* leave," she said sweetly, batting her eyelashes at him.

Crevan cringed at her flapping eyelashes and purposeful use of niceties. "This is my home, and you brought that thing in here! *I'm* not leaving."

Her eyes narrowed on him. "How dare you! I do as you ask, most of the time. How am I supposed to know the dealings of your realm when you so bloody loathe to speak to me and hear me ask questions? So take that flower and *be gone*!" she cried, her eyes brimming with tears. "Go back to your tranquil office you're so fond of. I'll finish here and be gone, our dealings can be finished so I will not disturb your precious life furthermore."

Gathering the bundles of flowers in her arms, she stormed off to a table in the farthest corner that held the least amount of light. Her heart felt as if a dagger was repeatedly stabbing it. Arabella thought, perhaps a bit too longingly, naively, or just insipidly wishful, that the brooding owner was coming round to her; that perhaps, she might find love in this beautiful and amazing world and, if not love, at least a place to belong. What she discovered was that she was just far too different for any of that to be obtainable.

In abject misery, Arabella hung her head, allowing the pooling tears to fall down her cold cheeks. She sniffed once, not ashamed of her frail human feelings, resolving to create a life for herself here since going back to where she came from might prove too perilous for her. She wasn't certain she could weather through another harsh London wintertide. Her meager belongings were probably in the possession of another by now. Arabella truly had nothing to her name. Higglehugh came up beside her, putting a small soft hand over top of hers, lending her a bit of warmth.

"I apologize for my dour mood, my friend," she said, heaving a sigh and drying her face with the back of her free hand. After a moment, Higglehugh stepped away, and she began to pick through the flowers, making colorful bundles. "I climbed The Wall between our worlds because I was misled. I grew up hearing everyone back in London telling tales of the faerie realm how dark, perilous, and frightening it was. What I found was such ethereal beauty, wondrous charm, and delight that I never knew was possible. Before I even set foot on Faerie's ground, a hooded figure enthralled me, stating that if I ate just one berry off a particular bush, my wildest dream would come true." She paused to smile wistfully at him. "Do you know what I wished for?"

Higglehugh shook his head as his periwinkle eyes observed her.

"A home," she confessed. "I wanted a house where I could rest under a roof free of leaks. A hearth to be warm and to bake bread. *A place to belong.* I was apprehended before I could make that ridiculous wish. The king turned me into a crow, telling me how I was now cursed into the form of the greediest animal in all of Faerie." She stopped, setting a bundle of flowers to the side.

"I would apologize again for my mood, though I fear it's frowned upon," Arabella told her friend. "If you wouldn't mind finding some tall vases for these flowers, I do believe that this task might be the final touch for your master."

Higglehugh nodded, trotting away to see to the task. Arabella leaned up against the table and squeezed her eyes tightly shut.

Crevan was right. I am a fool.

Chapter Nine

The Greater Fool

Crevan paced his office as he ran his finger through his copper strands, upsetting his carefully coiffed hair. His frustrations with the human girl boiled under his skin. Of course, it wasn't her fault the wiley creature made it inside. It was a sheer accident. How was she to know that leaving the door unlocked in Faerie would lead to such trouble? There were locks on their doors for a reason. He blew out a disheartened breath, more disappointed in himself. Why in all of Faerie did he tell her it was her fault? Because he needed to make her dislike him, hate him. She needed to know that he looked down on her, that her place was below him. But...his heart was bleeding, feeling as if he'd reached inside his own chest and savagely crushed it, proving that he was the greater fool. Arabella wasn't a pebble in his shoe. No, she was beginning to become his sunrise with her sarcastic wit and golden heart, such dualities that kept him on his toes.

An odd clattering sounded from above him. *What now?* Was his shoppe about to collapse around his pointed ears? A feminine yelp set his pulse racing. His feet sped him from the office to the front entrance; he breezed through the door, the distant chime of the bell seeming to float along the air behind him. Crevan's eyes took in his cottage as he quickly walked around to its side. There, he saw Higglehugh hanging from the middle rung of the ladder, and just above him, Arabella posed in the center of his roof on her hands and knees. Her eyes were locked on some object he couldn't quite see. Gingerly, she crawled forward and pulled the object toward her. Crevan shook his head at his mortal woman...*his woman*? Mortal or not, she wasn't *his* anything. Was she? Could she be? Now, with the dangers of either her slipping from the icy roof to land at his feet in a broken heap or Higglehugh letting go and plummeting to his demise, well, it wasn't the time to be thinking of what could be.

"I say, you are very studious, are you not? What could have fascinated you to such a degree that you risk life and limb to gather?" he shouted up at her with a puff of cloudy air leaving his mouth. With a start, Arabella began a slow slide from the eaves. Her free hand reached out to grasp onto anything with which to save herself, but besides the ladder, there wasn't anything for her to grab.

It took Crevan exactly two heartbeats before he ascended the ladder's step, steadying Higglehugh so that the dwarf could climb down to safety. After another few beats, he reached the last step and the thatched roof of the cottage. Arabella slid toward him. Crevan braced himself for impact, locking his knees to keep them both from falling as his hands came to her waist.

"I was doing very well. I didn't need rescuing," she said, avoiding eye contact with him as her breath frosted the air between them.

"Oh? Shall I leave you to it, then? Very well." He let her go, and she yowled in protest as her feet dangled over the roof's edge and the thing that she held to her chest nearly tumbled from her fingers.

"No, no," she swallowed as her hand patted his shoulder. "Since you're here, might as well make yourself useful. Help me down." Her bottom wiggled, causing a smirk of amusement to cross over his features.

"You are certain? You wouldn't like to remain here to...look at the stars? It's such a chilly evening, so perfect for a cozy interlude," he teased.

"A cozy interlude with you? I wouldn't dare impose myself upon you in such a manner. Why, it would be very debasing for you." Here, she began to shiver. By now, she was soaked through; her body heat had melted the ice.

Crevan focused on her lips and noted their blue hue. Flirting, if that was what he was doing, wasn't worth her discomfort; he was beginning to feel like a cad. The teasing smile vanished from his face and turned to somberness. Nodding to her, he reached for her center and drew her to him. She squealed and clung onto him, the fingertips of her free hand digging into the material of his tailcoat.

"Wrap your legs around my middle," he urged her.

A warm puff of air met his ear as she gasped, "That's highly improper!"

He chuckled, then replied, "So is a young lady roof-walking amid wintertide, but here we are."

"Fiiiiiine," she seethed, and with a most unladylike huff, she did as instructed.

Crevan began to stealthily descend the ladder as her warmth seeped into all the parts of himself that he kept such a tight rein upon. The minx was tying him up in the most complicated knots and he wasn't certain he could ever loosen them. He was startled when he realized that he liked the feel of her against him. Arabella fit him as no other ever had before. How could he ever let her go?

Crevan breathed a sigh of relief as they reached the ground. Tilting his head forward to peer down at his precious cargo, he saw that her eyes were tightly screwed shut. That was fine with him. He didn't really want to let her go. So he didn't. Higglehugh held the door open as he strode through it, proud as a peacock. Crevan felt ten feet tall, that she must have felt safe enough with him to let down her guard. Another shiver passed through her, and a sudden vice gripped his heart, for humans were not hearty creatures. A cold was enough to carry them to their graves, and he was determined that no such fate would befall the bewitching woman in his arms.

Speedily and with careful steps, Crevan strode toward his office with Arabella still in his arms, and he used his magic to unlock the door. Once through it, he rushed to the sofa and warily sat. Higglehugh followed after them and immediately began to stoke the fire. The room was a great deal warmer than out of doors, but it wasn't nearly warm enough to cast the chill from one's bones. When Higglehugh left them, it was to fulfill a request for Crevan's hot chocolate. The special brew was known to be a cure all. With Arabella still folded in his arms, Crevan rose and grabbed two pillows, which he conveyed to the open space just before the fire. After a moment, her teeth had stopped chattering, and he lowered himself to the floor atop one of the pillows.

After a time and with a deep sigh, Arabella pushed against his chest and tried to move away. The action ate at something vital in his heart.

"You must get warm," he cautioned her.

"I am a great deal warmer now. I can't sit in your lap all evening." She gave him a timid smile that wobbled. "Besides, you don't really desire me here. I'm a nuisance and—."

Ever-so-gently, he brought his forefingers under her jaw to keep her from breaking their gaze. Brows crashing together, he studied her for a moment before he spoke. Her skin was still pink from the chilly air, but thankfully the blue tint to it had disappeared. Her questioning eyes were luminous in the flickering light of the flame. He watched different emotions play out across her features. She was unsettled, uncertain of what this thing betwixt them was. He wanted to lay a hand over her smooth brow and caress the satiny skin along her cheekbone.

But would such liberties be welcomed? Or does she think that I am such an utter brute? Does she want nothing to do with me?

"I am not used to sharing my space," he began, gathering his courage. "I never was one of those nonsensical beings that chased after rainbows and happily-ever-afters. I was fine if I never came across the one who was meant for me. I'm not soft, not sentimental. I won't write you poetry nor sketch your likeness for hours unending. I don't know how to do those things. But I will treasure you above all others. I will reshape my entire world for you, doing my utmost to make your dreams mine. I'm gruff and rough even at the best of times, even when faced with a dream that I never allowed myself to entertain. I want to be better, to be changed, to be worthy of you. But it won't happen overnight. I am a creature of habit, and if there is to be something between us, that must change. Only tell me, do I have a chance of winning your hand? Even the slightest of hopes that you might, in time, come to care for me, faults and grumpiness aside?"

He felt raw and exposed to a degree that he had never allowed to happen before. But if he was to woo her, he knew in his heart that he must confess all to her. The good and the bad, and then let her decide their future, if indeed they had one.

Arabella's mouth popped open as her eyes fluttered. Emotions flitted across her luminous orbs while he waited with bated breath for her reply.

"Have I hit my head? Am I concussed?" Arabella's eyes misted as she intently stared at him.

"No, I do hope that's not a more preferable fate than me confessing my undying feelings for you."

A giggle slipped past her lips as she replied, "I am sorry to make you doubt me in this moment. This is like some hallucination, some imaginary happening. For my mind cannot wrap itself around your most beautiful and treasured words. If you want to know what my dream is, it's to make a home of my own."

"I see," he said, swallowing thickly and sniffing to banish the tears that wanted to shine in his eyes.

"You don't actually see, Crevan."

"And what don't I see?"

"Do you even know what the word 'home' means?"

Crevan guffawed. "*Pfft*, what a silly notion. It's where you rest your head, come in from the cold—."

"That's a house. A home is where your loved ones are, where a smile graces your face at the thought of being there with someone you love most. A home is where you sleep next to someone you cannot imagine living a second without and waking up to them each day. And I want to make a home with you."

"Oh, thank the Creator!" he nearly shouted, with the relief of the punishing weight sitting on his chest dissolving.

"You're certain that you want me? I seem to earn your ire readily enough, and I probably will spend my days doing so."

He softly chortled and threw his head back. "We are quite the pair, are we not?"

"I suppose we are," she answered as she snuggled against his chest, the delicate lace of his cravat tickling the supple flesh of her ear.

"Perchance in our imperfections, we may be perfectly happy together."

The door opened and Higglehugh bustled through with a silver serving tray that held two steaming mugs atop it.

"Took you long enough, chap," Crevan grumbled as he took a cup and handed it to his beloved.

Higglehugh winked at him, and Crevan grinned in return. Had the scamp purposefully left them alone?

Arabella gently placed the object she'd been holding onto into her lap. It was a bird's nest overbrimming with jewels and bits and bobbles. Meeting his eyes, she looked chagrin.

"Your trinkets from your adventure of being a feathered fowl?" He tried to hide his smile, but it burst free when she rolled her exquisite emerald eyes at him.

"Yes, I decided to retrieve it when I made up my mind to set out for even more adventures, this time on two feet. I was leaving just as soon as I had reclaimed them."

His face transformed into a brooding mask. "And do you still plan to leave?"

"What have we *just* been discussing, you silly fae? I'm most content exactly where I am, beside you. I'd be happier in your arms, but perhaps, if you've changed your mind, I should change mine?"

"Never! I shall never allow that to happen. You are mine, little mortal. We're as good as forever now."

"Truly? Isn't there some ceremony to bind us together like humans do with a wedding?" She looked at him with open curiosity.

"You let me attend to that matter," he promised as he brought her hand up to his mouth to press a delicate kiss along her silky skin.

Chapter Ten

Cupid Has Arrived

Crevan cautiously peeked out the kitchen door frame for the third time that morning. His little mortal was busy putting the final touches atop the tables before the confectionery opened for the holiday, *Valentine's Day.* He swallowed, thinking of the day that used to leave a sour taste in his mouth. This year *would* be different.

For the last three days Arabella had been fashioning doves and an assortment of hearts on little sticks to nestle between the beautiful arrangements of flowers. The effect was stunning. Watching her graceful movements and hearing her cheerful humming had lightened his heart and reaffirmed that he simply could never part from her. His happiness was intricately tied up in her. What would it be like once their bond was finally cemented?

These last days had been his most challenging as he endeavored to keep his project a secret from Arabella. Staying up half the night while his beloved slept on the sofa, Crevan crafted invitations to his most esteemed friends and family. It was a labor of love that would all be worth it very soon. This holiday, which Arabella had tried to play off as unimportant to her simply because she knew his prior feelings regarding it, would forevermore be cherished by them both.

He grinned, staring at his finished masterpiece. The five-tiered chocolate confection sported different layers of cake. Each layer boasted a different love scene—from kissing doves to heart-shaped macaroons, candied flowers to swans, to the finale at the top, which held decadent milk chocolate figurines of Crevan and Arabella. Each sumptuous layer of cake was a different variation of chocolate.

Crevan dusted his hands off on his green apron. "Well, old chap," he began to Higglehugh. "What do you think?"

The little dwarf clapped animatedly.

Crevan beamed happily. Whipping off his apron, he set it on the countertop. "Hide the masterpiece until the time is right," he instructed, trusting that the dwarf's magic would work splendidly.

Leaving the coziness of the kitchen, he strolled to the main section of his shoppe. Arabella's heart-shaped decor dangled from the ceiling, the floating fae lights making them glimmer under the rippling glow. The lovely bundles of flowers with hearts peeking out of them graced every tabletop. Much to Arabella's delight, he bespelled his dishes to give a soft peach color just for the holiday. She reached up onto her tiptoes and kissed his cheek when he had presented the enchantment to her.

Looking over his glass display case of goodies, he spied the sugared flowers and hearts he had been inspired to make just for the occasion. Cupcakes boasted red swans, their graceful necks twisted to peer behind them. Chocolate-dipped strawberries covered in delicate powdered sugar rested upon creamy strawberry cheesecake. He had even made delicate cake lollipops on sticks, each in the shape of a butterfly, and nestled them upon a smaller cake decorated to look like a field of flowers. And so, the holiday he once found disdainfully insipid became the holiday that brought him great joy.

Crevan took the special holiday menus out of their brass holder and nodded to Higglehugh to open the door for business. Once the small dwarf saw to the task, a giggling mass of fae came trotting through the open door, taking in all the new sights for the special day. He felt Arabella behind him, inhaling in a deep, stuttering breath.

"Once everyone is served, they'll be content. Fret not, my dear," Crevan said, shifting the menus to one hand and taking her hand in his other.

"I'm not panicking. I'm only hoping you made enough," she said, pulling her hand from his to gather her dark tresses back with a piece of pink ribbon he had given her that very morning after kissing the tip of her nose.

Crevan smirked, moving around behind her. He set the menus on the counter and tied the ribbon for her. "I have more in the ice storage in the kitchen."

"Thank you," she said. Once he was finished, she turned around to face him. No longer did he flinch at her gratitude; it was so intricately a part of who she was.

His breath caught in his lungs. The lovely, soft, rose empire-waisted dress bedecked in plum and silver roses accentuated her creamy skin tone and emerald eyes. If he was smiling at her, he couldn't remember when he had last done so, and so broadly. In fact, this woman made it impossible for him to do anything else *but* smile. Arabella made him realize that his heart had never felt so empty before her, and now, with her, he could never imagine life without her brilliance to shine upon him like dazzling sunbeams.

The boisterous atmosphere and general happiness of the establishment made his heart swell with pride as Crevan scanned the eager faces. He overheard his clientele gush over the human decor and the craft of his delicacies as he flitted around the room, filling orders while Arabella collected used plates and menus. Crevan had marked up the prices for the holiday confections per Arabella's instruction, stating she had seen something similar over the Faerie Wall. It was going so well he considered doing this again next year.

He grinned secretly behind the display glass as he once again returned to it, glancing about the room and noting that those he had sent a special invitation to had come. His family occupied the middle of the room. Among them were his beloved brother, his wife, and their darling kits. His best friend growing up, a renowned chef, waved his green webbed hand.

"Higglehugh," Crevan whispered in passing. "Crow's Nest!"

The quaint dwarf nodded determinedly, sprinting toward the kitchen and clapping his hands. Several other dwarfs emerged from the kitchen, tossing white rose petals out in front of the rolling cart. Arabella paused in gathering dishes to turn and look as the giant masterpiece made its grand appearance.

"How lovely!" Arabella exclaimed.

Crevan took the dishes from her and set them on the counter. He took Arabella's hand in his own, leading her to the middle of the room. Arabella eyed him suspiciously, delicate tendrils of her glorious hair falling out of the ribbon to frame her lovely face.

Grinning at her, he took a knee. Whipping out a piece of cream parchment, he cleared his throat. "The longest and shortest days are behind me because now I have you. The dreariest of nights and coldest of days are no longer because now I have you. The sun, the moon, the stars are all the clearer because now I have you. My dearest Arabella, you have made all my dreams come true." He paused, seeing her free hand fly up to cover the side of her face as tears trickled from her eyes. Crevan stood, removing her hand from her face to feel her soft skin against his own. "You are the very zest to my soul, the very beat to my heart. You are the one I have pined for all my life, and I cannot imagine another moment or a lifetime without you. My darling Arabella, will you marry me and bring light to all of our tomorrows?"

Arabella leaped into his arms, wrapping her body around his and completely crushing the parchment between them. "A thousand times, yes! An entire lifetime's worth!" She pulled back, untangling herself from him. "Is saying 'I love you' acceptable? Or is saying it something that will settle the charming frown upon your features?" Arabella teased as he stowed away the crumpled sheet and whipped a handkerchief from his waistcoat pocket, dabbing at her cheeks.

Refolding the linen, he looked deeply into her shining eyes. "Never when it pertains to you," he said, retrieving the filigree ring from another pocket and carefully slipping the jewel on her finger. "In Faerie, we don't have ceremonies or extravagant events when we pledge our hearts to one another. I only hope that this is sufficient to show you how much you truly mean to me."

"It's more than I ever dreamed. I love you, Crevan." Her brows furrowed as she leaned in to whisper, "What's your surname?"

"Sunbriar," he answered as the brightest smile bloomed. "And I love you, too, Missus Arabella Sunbriar."

The confectionery exploded with cheers and shouts of "Huzzah" and "Well done" as Crevan erased the few breaths of space separating his lips from hers. Lightning built in his heart as the golden glow of a ribbon tethering his heart wove its way to hers. First kisses were magical, and this one rivaled them all.

Epilogue

For Us

The excitement thrummed through Crevan's veins as Higglehugh ushered the last of the guests through the exitway. After the lovely afternoon, his impatience made it most difficult to be a good host and confectioner when all he longed to do was whisk Arabella away and share with his beloved all his secret projects. Now that the day was blessedly over, he could hardly stand to wait a moment more.

Once he heard Higglehugh lock the grinding bolt of the door, Crevan took his wife by the hand and led her to the office, past the flowers that filled the air with fragrance and the hanging hearts that twirled in the air. Waving his hand, his golden magic revealed a secret door just to the right of the office entry.

"Has that always been there?" Arabella asked, canting her head.

Chuckling, Crevan answered her, "No, for this is a fairly new addition. For we had no living quarters, no space to receive guests, and perhaps the most important of all...no bed."

"Oh," she replied as a delicate blush infused her cheeks.

Gently, he tugged her through the doorway and up the flight of polished wooden steps. At the top of the stairway stood three separate doors. Opening the first one to their right, waving his palm to light the chamber, he waited with bated breath to see her reaction.

Arabella unbraided their fingers and trod into the bedchamber. It was furnished in burgundy with golden accents, a settee placed before a marble fireplace, a rosewood dressing table, and a matching padded bench. And, of course, the focal point was the four-poster bed piled high with pillows. Dark curtains were drawn over a window that overlooked the front of the cottage. Her face lit up, and tears sprang to her eyes.

"You like it?" he asked as he ran an anxious hand through his auburn hair.

"I don't merely like it, Crevan; I adore it!" she exclaimed as she lovingly ran her hand over the silver brush atop the dressing table.

"I have more to show you."

Arabella retraced her steps and allowed him to lead her to the last chamber, bypassing the middle one completely. She perked a brow at him as he twisted the doorknob and pushed the door open. A gasp left her mouth, and she rushed into the center of the sitting room. A matching set of ivory sofas faced each other, and a rocking chair stood just before a fireplace. Fresh blossoms were set about in tall vases at each corner, and lanterns rested upon beautiful mahogany end tables. A crystal chandelier hung from the very middle of the chamber, casting rainbowed light onto the furnishings and Aubusson rug.

"This pleases you?" Crevan asked from behind her, folding her in his arms. She leaned her head back against his chest.

"You know it does," she softly whispered.

"Why are you whispering?"

"Because I am scared to believe that this isn't some dream. If it is, I don't ever want to wake."

He let her go and came to stand in front of her. Lowering himself to meet her eyes, he said, "You have no need to fear. This is real. It's you and me." He caressed her satiny cheek. "It's true that love like this doesn't happen every day. But believe me, you have nothing to fear."

Grasping her hand in his, he pulled her tenderly from the room and back to the middle door. Once it was open, he walked in with her tucked into his arm. Inside was an oak rocking horse, a mahogany cradle, a three-story dollhouse, and ten tiny tin soldiers standing sentry along the mantle of the fireplace. Pale blue curtains hung over the windows, and silk-papered walls boasted little wispy clouds. It was the most beautiful and inviting chamber in the entire cottage.

Arabella breathlessly asked him, "You did this for me?"

"I did this for us."

"For us," she echoed. "But when? How?"

"This is what I have spent the majority of my time constructing with the help of the dwarfs. I'm as rich as Croesus and it was well past time to put my savings to good use. I could think of nothing better than making a home for you, for us."

"You're extraordinary. But you already know that," she teased, and she reached up to tickle the underside of his jaw with light kisses.

Could life be any brighter, any sweeter? He could bake and enchant all day long and never find anything more savory than a life to live by her side, their fingers woven together, and her heart ribboned to his.

About Michelle Helen Fritz

Michelle Helen Fritz was born in Maryland and raised in Arizona with lots of traveling throughout the States. She began her literary career as a personal assistant to Indie authors and loves to see the process of an idea turn into a finished book. Michelle loves to write about dashing heroes and the compelling women that tempt them with a dash of intrigue, an abundant amount of romance, and scenes that hopefully make her readers swoon. She is the mother of four children whom she homeschools and currently resides in Maryland with her own jaunty hero who makes all of her dreams come true.

You can follow Michelle on:

Amazon Author Page: Michelle Helen Fritz

Facebook: Author Michelle Helen Fritz

Instagram: Author Michelle Helen Fritz

Acknowledgements

We have to thank our beta readers for helping to polish this to a perfect shine! Thank you endlessly Brittany, Cathey, J.J. and Lisa! We adore each of you!

Thank you so very much to Wanderlust Ink & Tomb L.L.C. for creating such a fabulous cover! We are tickled pink!

This story would not exist if T.S. had not invited us along! We have had such a fabulous time creating these stories for the anthologies and it's been an honor to be included!

Thank you, to you, dear reader! We are so excited that you chose to read our story. If you were happily whisked away to Faerie, we would love to read your thoughts in a review.

Lastly, a huge well of gratitude to our families. Thank you for all the things!

Also by: Michelle Helen Fritz

A Bramley Hall Regency Romance

Love At Last

Love That Lasts

Love Ever Lasting

Shades of Bramley Hall Regency Romance

Love Holds True

Courts & Curses

A Court Of Broken Dreams and Curse

A Court of Broken Promises and Nightmares

A Court of Broken Hopes and Wishes

Paullett Golden Anthology

Hourglass Romance: *Love At Rescue*

Romantic Choices: *Love Flames Anew*

Romantic Realms Anthology

Hearts At War: *Faerie Boots*

Shifting Hearts: *Faeriely Tart*

Beyond The Depths Anthology

A Bite of Winter & A Sip of Trouble: *Faerie Wishes*

About E.A. Shanniak

E.A. (Ericka Ashlee) Shanniak is the author of several successful series – A Castre World Novel – Whitman Western Romances – Dangerous Ties. She's hobbit-sized, barely reaching over 5ft tall on a good day. When she wears her Ariat boots, not only does she gain an inch, she's then able to reach the kitchen cabinets to get all the snacks. When not in her fox den (writing cave), Ericka loves to spend time with her family – outside having firepits with wine, camping, fishing, or zooming in her jeep on another Midwest adventure. Ericka loves all the animals her kids bring home including numerous barn cats and their newfound duck named Delilah.

Ericka works in the Register of Deeds office residing in a small town in Comanche County with her supportive, wonderful husband, two amazingly compassionate kids, and all the animals (including those her husband knows nothing about yet). Follow her on her Kansas adventures with these social media platforms listed below.

- Facebook

- Facebook group: Shanniak Shenanigans
- Instagram

website: http://www.eashanniak.com/

email: erickashanniak@gmail.com

If you have a moment, I would really appreciate a review. A review, whether you liked it or not, helps me know what aspects of the story you liked. Even a rating is helpful. Thank you so much for reading my work. I hope you have a fabulous day.

Also by: E.A. Shanniak

Clean Fantasy Romance – Zerelon World Novella:

Aiding Azlyn

Killing Karlyn

Reviving Roslyn

Clean & Sweet Regency Romance – Bramley Hall:

Love At Last

Love That Lasts

Love Ever Lasting

Clean & Sweet Western Romance – Whitman Western Series:

To Find A Whitman

To Love A Thief

To Save A Life

To Lift A Darkness

To Veil A Fondness
To Bind A Heart
To Hide A Treasure
To Want A Change
To Form A Romance

Harlequin Fantasy Romance – Castre World Novel:
Piercing Jordie
Mitering Avalee
Forging Calida
Uplifting Irie
Braving Evan
Warring Devan
Hunting Megan
Shifting Aramoren – *short story*
Anchoring Nola – *short story*

Slow Burn Enemies to Lovers Paranormal Romance – Dangerous Ties:
Opening Danger
Hunting Danger
Burning Danger

Slow Burn Enemies to Lovers Paranormal Romance – Wicked Ties:
Wicked Witch
Wicked Bonds
Wicked Ruin

Standalone Stories:
Winter Luna